MAINE COONS

MARYSA STORM

Black Rabbit Books

Bolt Jr. is published by Black Rabbit Books
P.O. Box 227, Mankato, Minnesota, 56002.
www.blackrabbitbooks.com
Copyright © 2025 Black Rabbit Books

Alissa Thielges, editor
Rhea Magaro, designer

All rights reserved. No part of this book may be reproduced in any form without written permission from the publisher.

Names: Storm, Marysa, author.
Title: Maine coons / by Marysa Storm.
Description: Mankato, MN : Black Rabbit Books, [2025] | Series: Bolt Jr. Our favorite cats | Includes bibliographical references and index. | Audience: Ages 5–8 | Audience: Grades K–1
Identifiers: LCCN 2024010401 (print) | LCCN 2024010402 (ebook) | ISBN 9781644666784 (library binding) | ISBN 9781644666968 (ebook)
Subjects: LCSH: Maine coon cat—Juvenile literature.
Classification: LCC SF449.M34 S767 2025 (print) | LCC SF449.M34 (ebook) | DDC 636.8/3—dc23/eng/20240424
LC record available at https://lccn.loc.gov/2024010401
LC ebook record available at https://lccn.loc.gov/2024010402

Image Credits

Shutterstock/AlinArt, 15, AVRORACOON, 18, DenisNata 1, DragoNika, 12, Elena Butinova, 13, Eric Isselee, 4, 7, 21, Jela Skolkova, 23, Kukurund, cover, Nils Jacobi, 20–21, Nynke van Holten, 8–9, Okeanas, 11, Olleg Visual Content, 5, Polina Tomtosova, 3, 24, Pony3000, 19, Roland IJdema, 10, Sherbak_photo, 17, Summer, 1810, 6

Contents

Chapter 1
Meet the Maine Coon 4

Chapter 2
Personality 10

Chapter 3
Maine Coon Care 16

More Information 22

CHAPTER 1

Meet the Maine Coon

A large cat **slinks** into the bathroom. It is a Maine Coon. Its owner is filling the tub. Bath time! Interested, the cat jumps in. Splash! Its long fur gets wet. But this cat doesn't mind. It wants to play.

slink: to move in a sneaky way

COMPARING SIZES

Maine Coon
8 to 18 pounds
(4 to 8 kg)

Large Cats

Maine Coons are big. In fact, they are the biggest type of housecat. They grow bigger than some small dogs! They have large, tufted ears. Their tails are long and fluffy.

▶ **Yorkshire terrier**
Less than 7 pounds (3 kg)

PARTS OF A Maine Coon

eyes

long coat

CHAPTER 2
Personality

Maine Coons are often called **gentle** giants. They like to relax with their owners. They get along well with kids and other pets.

gentle: kind and quiet

FACT

Maine Coons like playing in water.

11

Smart Cats

These cats are curious. They love to climb around. They are also **clever**. Their owners can teach them tricks. Some even learn how to play fetch.

clever: smart and able to learn quickly

Where They Come From

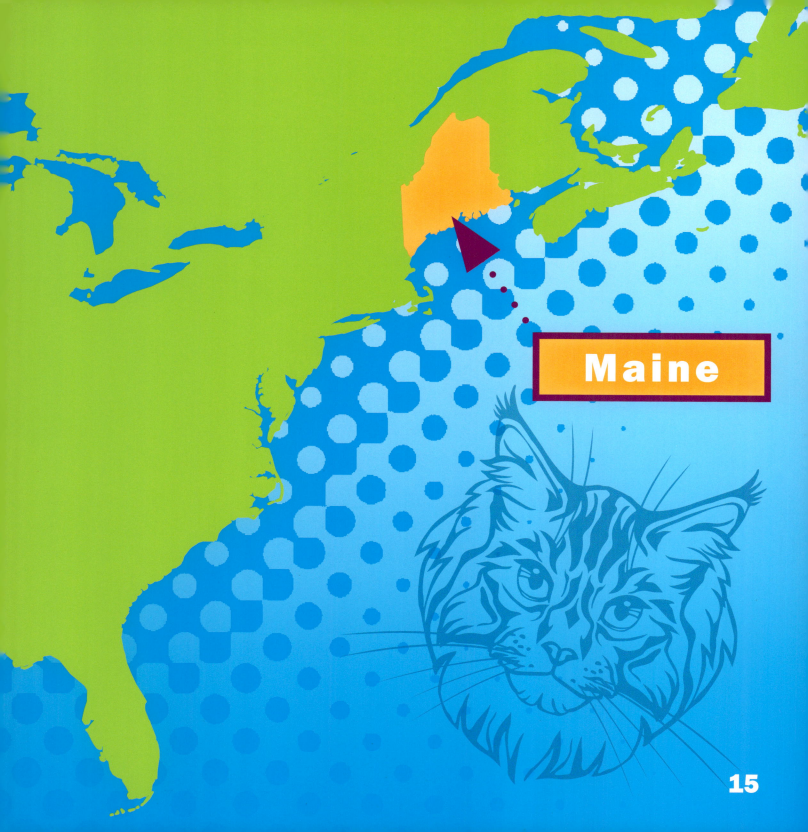

CHAPTER 3

Maine Coon Care

Maine Coons love to play. It is an easy way to keep them active. And it makes them happy.

These cats also need their nails trimmed regularly. They need to be brushed once a week. Their long coats can get tangled.

FACT

A Maine Coon's tail is as long as its body.

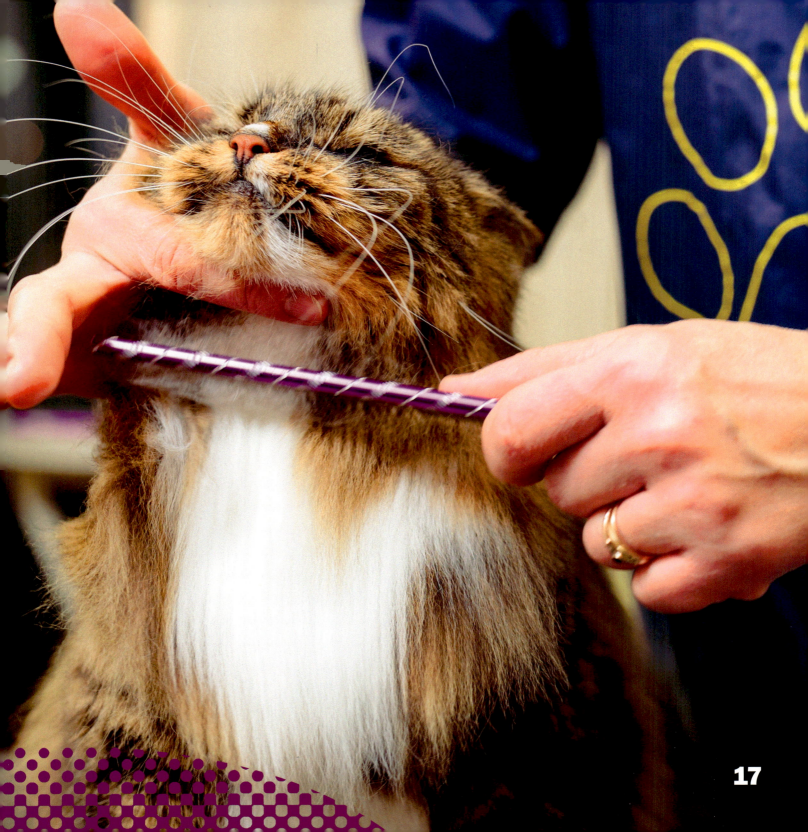

Friendly Felines

These big cats are good first pets. They need plenty of attention. And their coats need lots of brushing. But people say they are worth it. They make great furry friends.

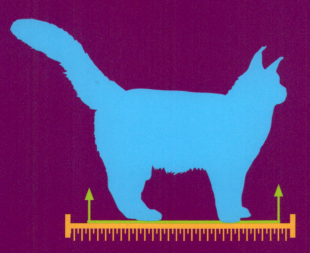

Maine Coon's Length
up to 3 feet
(91 centimeters)

Bonus Facts

Most Maine Coons are brown tabbies.

tabby: a cat with dark and light stripes or spots

Their eyes are often gold, green, or brownish.

Their coat is **ticked**.

They live up to **15 years**.

ticked: bands of color on a strand of hair that are darker at the tip

READ MORE/WEBSITES

Andrews, Elizabeth. *Maine Coon Cats.* Minneapolis: Cody Koala, an imprint of Pop!, 2023.

Burling, Alexis. *Cats.* Minneapolis: Abdo Publishing Company, 2024.

Kissock, Heather. *Maine Coon.* New York: Lightbox Learning Inc., 2023.

Maine Coon Cat
www.ducksters.com/animals/maine_coon_cat.php

Maine Coon Cat
kids.britannica.com/students/article/Maine-coon-cat/312313

State Cat – Maine Coon Cat
www.maine.gov/sos/kids/about/symbols/cats

GLOSSARY

clever (KLEV-er)—smart and able to learn quickly

gentle (JEN-tuhl)—kind and quiet

slink (SLINGK)—to move in a sneaky way

tabby (TAH-bee)—a cat with dark and light stripes or spots

INDEX

B
body parts, 7, 8–9, 16, 21

C
care, 16, 19
colors, 20

I
intelligence, 13

L
life span, 21

O
origin, 14-15

P
personality, 4, 10, 16

S
size, 6–7, 19